For Lisa Seiberling and Judy DiPietro,
who taught me the magic mysteries
of elementary schools
J. P. L.


To the memory of Bayli
B. A.

Published by Dial Books for Young Readers
A division of Penguin Putnam Inc.
345 Hudson Street, New York, New York 10014
Text copyright © 2001 by J. Patrick Lewis
Pictures copyright © 2001 by Brian Ajhar
Poems in this collection that have been previously published are:
"First Men on the Moon," in *Lives: Poems About Famous Americans,* HarperCollins, 1999,
edited by Lee Bennett Hopkins, and in *Creative Classroom,* 1999.
"First Parachute Wedding," in *Light Quarterly,* 1999.
Designed by Lily Malcom
Printed in Hong Kong on acid-free paper
10 9 8 7 6 5 4 3 2 1

Library of Congress Cataloging-in-Publication Data
Lewis, J. Patrick.
A burst of firsts: doers, shakers, and record breakers/
by J. Patrick Lewis; pictures by Brian Ajhar.
p.    cm.
Summary: A collection of poems that celebrate such notable firsts as
the first American woman in space, the first king of rock 'n' roll, the first man
to run a four-minute mile, and the first person to make blue jeans.
ISBN 0-8037-2108-0
1. Curiosities and wonders—Juvenile poetry. 2. World records—Juvenile poetry.
3. Children's poetry, American. [1. American poetry.] I. Ajhar, Brian, ill. II. Title.
PS3562.E9465B87    2001
811'.54—dc21              99-44286         CIP

*The art was prepared using watercolors, watercolor pencils,
acrylic paint and glazes, colored pencils, ink, and airbrush.*

# A BURST OF FIRSTS

## Doers, Shakers, and Record Breakers

by J. Patrick Lewis
pictures by Brian Ajhar

Dial Books for Young Readers  New York

# The Biggest Bubble-Gum Bubble Ever Blown

*23 inches wide • Fresno, California • July 19, 1994*

Susan Montgomery Williams one day
Had nothing to do when she went out to play,
So she took out some gum
And she started to chew
And to chew and to chew.
(Like a panda bear munching
A stalk of bamboo.)

And Susan Montgomery
Williams just knew
If she blew and she blew
And she blew and she blew,
She'd pop the world gum-blowing
Record in two!

And the bubble? It grew
And it grew and it grew
Until it had grown a foot wide,
And then ... two!
If bubble gum blowers
Belonged in *Who's Who*,
They'd add Ms. Montgomery Williams—
That's Sue!

# First Non-Japanese Sumo Wrestler

*Akebono (Chadwick Haheo Rowan)*
*Promoted to the top rank of*
*Yokozuna (sumo wrestler) in 1993*

What's even more surprising than
    The belly of a sumo
Wrestler is his very, very
    *Miniature* costume! Oh,
You must assume a sumo wears
    A regular bikini,
But everything about him screams
    The *opposite* of teeny!

# First Parachute Wedding

*Ann Hayward and Arno Rudolphi*
*World's Fair, New York City • August 25, 1940*

Suspended there
Above the Fair,
A bride and groom
And love...in bloom.

The best man swayed
Beside the maid
Of honor who
Admired the view.

Humanity
Looked up to see
The strings of four
Musicians soar.

The preacher said,
"I do thee wed."
These high-flown words
Alarmed the birds.

The couple kissed
(But mostly missed)
Until they floun-
dered to the ground.

From skies above
They fell...in love.
Her wedding vow?
A simple *"Wow!"*

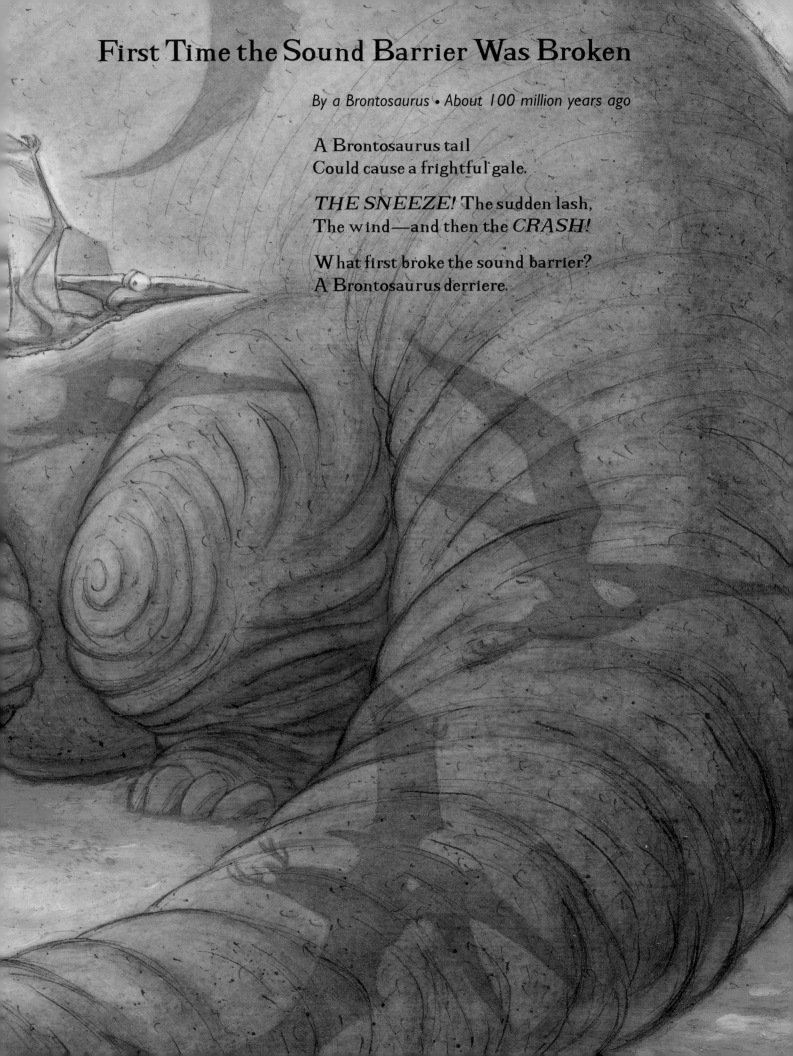

# First Time the Sound Barrier Was Broken

*By a Brontosaurus • About 100 million years ago*

A Brontosaurus tail
Could cause a frightful gale.

*THE SNEEZE!* The sudden lash,
The wind—and then the *CRASH!*

What first broke the sound barrier?
A Brontosaurus derriere.

# First Men on the Moon

*"The Eagle has landed!"* —Apollo 11 Commander Neil A. Armstrong
*"A magnificent desolation!"* —Air Force Colonel Edwin E. "Buzz" Aldrin, Jr.
*July 20, 1969*

That afternoon in mid-July,
Two pilgrims watched from distant space
The moon ballooning in the sky.
They rose to meet it face-to-face.

Their spidery spaceship, *Eagle*, dropped
Down gently on the lunar sand.
And when the module's engines stopped,
Rapt silence fell across the land.

The first man down the ladder, Neil,
Spoke words that we remember now—
"One small step..." It made us feel
As if we were there too, somehow.

When Neil planted the flag and Buzz
Collected lunar rocks and dust,
They hopped like kangaroos because
Of gravity. Or wanderlust?

A quarter million miles away,
One small blue planet watched in awe.
And no one who was there that day
Will soon forget the sight they saw.

# #1 Lunch Choice of School Kids

ISN'T macaroni
ISN'T French fries
ISN'T plain bologna
ISN'T Moon Pies
ISN'T peanut butter
ISN'T Cap'n Crunch
ISN'T what your mother went
And packed inside your lunch!

IS a wheel of pastry
Cut up into wedges,
Steaming hot tomato paste
Spread up to the edges,
Sausage, pepperoni, ham,
Mozzarella cheese,
IS a present for your mouth!
Pass the *PIZZA*, please!

# First King of Rock 'n' Roll

*Elvis Presley • 1935–1977*

Elvis Presley, swinging star,
Shook his hips when he played guitar.
Somebody said they saw his car
Parked outside The Go-Go.

Elvis, Elvis, I heard tell
Booked the whole Heartbreak Hotel,
Greased his hair with Elvis gel,
Just to play The Go-Go.

Elvis, Elvis, dressed in black
Went to heaven, but he just came back!
Gave me a ride in his pink Cadillac,
Cruisin' past The Go-Go.

# First Lady of Twentieth-Century Sports

*Mildred "Babe" Didrikson Zaharias • 1914–1956*

Let me tell you a little story
   About Babe Zaharias.
She walked like you and she talked like me,
   But she wasn't like any of us.

She was born in outback Texas,
   Where the tallest tall tales grow,
And they stood in line to see her
   One-superwoman show.

Babe raced the wind and beat it,
   She high-hurdled the town,
She threw the javelin a mile—
   And caught it coming down.

Babe long-jumped over Texas,
   And put the shot so far,
It flew over Oklahoma
   Just like a shooting star.

And when she took up golfing,
   She had seventeen straight wins.
That's where the lady's story ends—
   And her legend then begins.

# First Man to Win the Heavyweight Boxing Title Three Times

*Muhammad Ali • b.1942*

How sweet
The buzz
   Inside the ring
Until
Ali,
   The Bee, would sting.

The dancing
Butterfly
   Burned bright
At the cham-
   Pionship
      Title fight.

Across
The world
   They shout his name
Because
He made
   The world his game.

# First Recorded 6,000-Year-Old Tree in America

*The "Eon Tree" • A coast redwood*
*Humboldt County, California*
*250 feet tall • about 6,200 years old*

When Mother Nature held her ground,
When almost no one was around,
A redwood bud began to grow
And watch the seasons come and go.

For sixty centuries or more,
It stood upon the forest floor
And waved its arms about the sky
And sang a woodland lullaby.

December 1977:
The Eon Tree, so tall to heaven,
Bowed gracefully and bid farewell
To all its fellow-trees,

                              *and fell.*

# First Child to Integrate an All-White School

*Ruby Bridges*
*William Frantz Elementary School*
*New Orleans, Louisiana • 1960*

They called me names.
The words got worse,
words that slice the bone
like Mama's peeling knife.
*Git on, nappy,* they'd curse,
*you don't belong,*
        *go with your kind.*

But I left hate behind,
and walked with the marshals
into a big white room
e m p t y
    r o a r i n g
        s i l e n t
as a tomb.

Weeks went by.
White kids looking in
Would shy away from me like
            sin.

Mrs. Henry
taught me wonder,
taught me right,
taught me nothing
is ever
    simply
        BLACK and WHITE.

# First Girls in Little League Baseball

*December 26, 1974*
*Title IX of the 1972 Education Act is signed, providing for equal opportunity in athletics for girls as well as boys.*

The year was 1974
When Little Leaguers learned the score.
President Ford took out his pen,
And signed a law that said from then
On women too would have the chance
To wear the stripes and wear the pants.
Now what you hear, as flags unfurl,
Is "Atta boy!" and "Atta girl!"

# First African American Female to Win the Nobel Prize for Literature

*Toni Morrison*
*b. Chloe Anthony Wofford, in 1931*

*The Bluest Eye*
   Will let you see.
Books get you by,
   They set you free.

The stories gleam.
   The heat, the sweat
Undaze a dream
   You can't forget.

*Sula, Beloved,*
   *Solomon, Jazz,*
And *Paradise* proved
   What gifts she has.

# First Person to Create Blue Jeans

*Levi Strauss • San Francisco • 1873*

First, coal miners wore the pants.
(Denim came from southern France.)
Cowboys followed, then came teens—
Half the world is wearing jeans.

You decide which pair you want—
Zipper-fly or button-front,
Loose-fit, wide-leg, classic kind …
Half the world's been redesigned,
*Sew* it *seams*, on its behind.

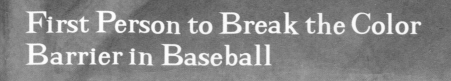

# First Person to Break the Color Barrier in Baseball

*Jackie Robinson • 1919–1972*
*Joined the Brooklyn Dodgers in 1947*

Inching along the third-base line,
the Prince of Easy Afternoons
would suddenly explode for home
in the astonished air.
His was an American joy.
When you saw him for the first time,
you waited   waited   waited
under a crackerjack sky
for the dashing black player

            *… to fly.*

# First Man to Win Springboard- and Platform-Diving Gold Medals in Two Olympics

*Greg Louganis*
*1984 and 1988*

Platform looks out on the town,
inward pike
ten meters
down.

Springboard sends me to the sky,
forward tuck
three meters
high.

Twisting jacknife,

make a wish—

way out lay out entry

sspppplli i iissshh

# First Person to Go Over Niagara Falls in a Barrel—and Survive

*Anna Edson Taylor • Horseshoe Falls • October 24, 1901*

How many dare-
Devils had tried
Niagara Falls?
How many died

Before a woman,
Forty-three,
Set out to test
The powers that be?

Her wooden barrel,
Set adrift
Above the Falls,
Soon met the swift

White-crested waves
Where others, brief-
ly pitched and tossed,
Had come to grief.

And like a bobber
Far from shore,
Her barrel plunged
Across the roar

Of history.
In mist and steam,
Her little house
Was swept downstream.

The rescue party
Was amazed
To find the daring
Woman dazed

But still alive!
What did she say?
"How blessed I am
To see this day."

# First House of Cards With More Than 500 Decks

*Built by Bryan Berg • More than 27,000 cards*
*Spirit Lake, Iowa • February 24–March 3, 1995*

There was a young man who built him a house,
And this was the house that jacks built.

It had 83 stories
With 83 doors
And 83 ceilings,
So how many floors
Of twos-by-twos
And threes-by-fours?

No glues, no screws, no special effects
Used by conventional architects,
Just playing cards—*more than 500 decks!*
And this was the house that jacks built.

About 6,000 cards
Had pictures of faces.
There were 2,000 deuces,
So how many aces
Were ceilings and floors
In various places?

There was a young man who built him a house,
And this was the house that jacks built,
That kings and queens and sevens and fours
And nines and eights and jacks built.

# First Man to Run a Four-Minute Mile

*Roger Bannister • Oxford, England • May 6, 1954 • 3:59.4 minutes*

Though Oxford clouds undid the day—
A chill kept many fans away—
The "dream mile" was a splendid race!
Young Brasher set the early pace
By going out extremely fast.
His teammates knew he wouldn't last,
And Chataway took the lead, as planned,
Just as they passed the viewing stand.
The half? 1:58.2!
At every curve the promise grew
That this day might be destiny.

And Roger Bannister knew that he
Could leap into the future, so
With some three hundred yards to go,
Began his kick, his head rolled back,
Pounding to glory down the track.
His body honed to perfect shape,
He won, collapsing at the tape!
And gave the credit to a team
That chased a boy who chased a dream.
He said, as history would tell,
"I did one thing supremely well."

# First Person Who Jumped Rope More Than 14,000 Times in One Hour

*Park Bong Tae • Pusan, South Korea*
*14,628 jumps in one hour • July 2, 1989*

**W**oodpecker, woodpecker, **y**ep, that's **me**!
Okay, **y**ou be the **c**hickadee-**dee**!
**J**ump in, **j**aybird, **h**op along, **wren**,
**T**wirl in, **h**ummingbird, 'round a**gain**.
**F**ly away, **h**ummingbird, **j**aybird, **wren**,
**W**oodpecker, **c**hickadee—**o**ut a**gain**!

The rope turners twirl the rope at medium speed, hitting
the ground on the four bold letters in each line.

◆ ◆ ◆ ◆ ◆

Feet that feel good fly
Toes that feel good tap
Hands that feel good clap
Fingers that feel good snap
Arms that feel good swing
Lungs that feel good sing
Heels that feel good click
Legs that feel good kick
Eyes that feel good wink
Heads that feel good think
Feet that feel good fly
Off the ground.
**Good-bye!**

# First Man to Lead the NBA in Scoring for Ten Years

*Michael Jordan • b.1963*

Michael

Jordan—

Just

An

Ordin-

Ary

**Guy**

In

The

Sky.

# First American Woman in Space

*Sally K. Ride • Astronaut • b.1951*
*First space flight on June 18, 1983*

Sally Ride rode
An alley-wide road
Into the sky.

Sally Ride rode
To an area code
A million miles high.

Sally Ride rode
With a precious payload
Out of Earthsight.

Sally Ride rode
Sally Ride Road
Into the night.